Prudy
at Meadows Farm

Story and Pictures by
Decie Merwin

Originally titled *Pink-Tails*

TABLE OF CONTENTS

Cover design by Elle Staples
Cover illustration by Nada Serafimovic and
Decie Merwin

First published in 1950
This unabridged version has updated
spelling and punctuation.

For
Miss Mary Aston
with deep affection

MEADOWS FARM

PRUDY TAIT'S HAIR DIDN'T CURL A BIT, BUT Prudy didn't mind. It was the color of silver-gilt, and Mother braided it in two stubby little braids that just brushed her shoulders. Prudy loved them. She called them her "pink-tails," and, sure enough, they were tied with pale pink ribbons that just matched the color of Prudy's cheeks.

Sometimes her dresses were checked, and sometimes they were plain, but always they were a blue that just matched Prudy's eyes.

And she wore pinafores.

The pinafores were span-clean in the morning and crisp with starch. By evening they were limp and badly smudged.

Mother sighed and brought a clean, crisp pinafore from the kitchen where the ironing board was still up.

"Some little girls wear denim shorts," she said, "when they play in the park, anyway—or overalls."

"Not overalls," said Prudy's father. "Not on my daughter. I like little girls to *be* little girls, not tomboys."

So Mother tied on the fresh pinafore, and Prudy smoothed it neatly, and they all sat down to supper.

Prudy's father tweaked a "pink-tail."

"You look sweet enough to eat," he said. "Like sugar and spice and everything nice—the way little girls should."

⁂

That was before Prudy went to visit the farm.

She was to stay without Mother and Daddy for the first time while they went off on a little holiday of their own.

It was Granny's farm.

But a lot of people seemed to live there besides Granny.

They all came out to meet her when Daddy and Mother and Prudy drove up in the car.

There were greetings, much laughter, and talk.

"You see, darling, you can't possibly be lonesome," Mother said brightly. "All your cousins to play with—such fun! And Auntie May will help with dressing or anything if Granny is busy."

"And we'll be back in two short weeks," Daddy said. "Why, you'll hardly know that we're gone!"

"You're really a big girl now—when you're big enough to visit by yourself."

They kissed her.

They waved.

They drove away.

Prudy didn't feel like a big girl.

She felt very small.

She looked at her cousins. They were all much bigger than she was.

She looked at the house. It was the biggest house she had ever seen. It stood among the tallest trees.

Her own suitcase, on the path beside her, looked very large.

One of her cousins, a big boy with red hair and freckles, picked it up.

"Gee," he said. "What's in this thing? Rocks?"

"My—my clothes," said Prudy.

Her voice quavered a little.

Granny laughed.

"It is a big suitcase for such a small girl, but I guess you're strong enough to carry it upstairs, Spotty. Or Tucker can help you."

She turned to Prudy.

"You come with me, child," she said. "We'll go up to your room. It's a tiny one next to mine. Your mother used to sleep there when she was your size. I think you'll love it."

And Prudy did.

Not only was the room tiny, but the ceiling sloped down into the wall on each side of the window. The bed and the little dressing table were painted white, and there were snowy, ruffled curtains with pink rosebuds on them. There was wallpaper with pink roses, too—just the color of the ribbons that tied Prudy's "pink-tails."

Outside the window were the green branches of a big tree, and outside the door was Granny's big bedroom. This made the little room seem even smaller, just the right size for a little girl.

Prudy didn't say anything, but she went around the room touching the pink roses and smiling, and she felt sure Granny knew how much she liked it.

They went downstairs where Prudy had a glass of milk that tasted better than the milk in town— and sugar cookies to go with it.

Her cousins were very nice to her.

They showed her the old spring house, cool and damp.

And the corn crib.

And the big, red, dusty barn.

There were animals in the barn: a few hens, a cow with a little brown-eyed calf, two great *big* horses, and a gray pony.

Prudy asked questions.

Tommy and Tucker said, "Didn't you know that?" and "Didn't you know *that*?"

And Midge looked surprised.

But Spotty told her everything.

He showed her how to feed carrots to the big farm horses—flat on her palm so they couldn't make a mistake and nibble a finger instead of a carrot. He let her take a warm brown egg from a hen's nest that was hidden away in the hay.

And he gave her a ride on the gray pony!

The pony's back was round and slippery, but she grabbed his thick mane with both hands, and Spotty led him carefully. First, they walked. Then they trotted. Prudy's cheeks got pinker and pinker. She lost a ribbon, and one of her "pink-tails" came undone. Her little blue skirt flopped up and down,

and the strings of her pinafore untied and trailed behind her like the tail of a kite.

"Hang on, now," Spotty told her. He started to run, and they came back to the barn at a canter.

Prudy squealed with delight. She had never had such fun.

Spotty lifted her down.

Midge got on the pony and galloped around the lawn without anybody leading. Midge was wearing blue jeans, and she didn't seem to find the pony's back slippery at all.

Prudy watched her. She thought Midge was wonderful.

All her cousins were wonderful.

And she liked Spotty the best.

They played hide-and-seek in the barn.

Prudy's dress got torn. So did her pinafore.

A bell rang, and they ran pell-mell for the house. Prudy couldn't run as fast as the others, but Spotty waited for her.

Spotty was her favorite cousin.

"Goodness, child!" Granny said when she saw Prudy. "Goodness! Well, it'll do you good. Your cheeks look pinker already. Only, I'm afraid that frock and pinny are beyond mending."

The children had supper on the porch. They played tag among the trees on the grassy lawn.

They caught fireflies and let them go again.

Then it was time for bed.

When Prudy woke the next morning, Granny was standing in the doorway with a small pair of faded blue jeans in her hand.

"I guess these will do," she said. "One of the children outgrew them. They're patched, but I couldn't find anything in your suitcase that wouldn't be ruined in ten minutes on a farm. Hop up now, and I'll help you dress."

Prudy hopped.

"Shall I braid your hair or let it fly?" asked Granny.

"Oh, braid it, Granny. I do want my pink-tails, please."

Prudy felt strange enough as she looked down at her legs in the blue jeans with a patch on one knee. She didn't want her head to feel strange, too.

Granny gave her breakfast on a corner of the kitchen table.

"I'm working butter on the back porch," she said. "You can come out and watch me when you've finished."

Prudy wondered where her cousins were. She felt a little lonely in spite of thick cream on her cereal and brown honey for her biscuit.

But it was fun to see the glass churn with its whirling paddle and, after it stopped, to watch Granny knead and press the milk out of the lump of pale golden butter.

"Just the color of your pink-tails, isn't it?" Granny smiled.

"My pink-tails are silver-gilt."

"Silver-gilt in town—butter-colored in the country," said Granny. "It's much the same."

She pressed the butter into a wooden mold, and it came out with a little strawberry picture on top.

Prudy liked watching, but she still wondered about her cousins. Finally, she asked Granny.

"Where—where are the others?"

"The children? Oh, the boys went fishing, I think. And Midge drove into the village with your Aunt May."

"Oh—"

Perhaps little girls didn't go fishing.

Prudy thought about her cousins for a few minutes.

"They've got funny names, haven't they, Granny? All of them."

"Oh, those are nicknames, of course," Granny said. "Nicknames always happen in a big family that's on good terms with itself. It's a part of the give and take, I guess—a sort of good-natured teasing. Shows they like each other."

Prudy sighed. It would be nice, she thought, to be one of a big family and have a nickname. She wasn't quite sure what teasing was like, but she wouldn't mind, she thought, if Spotty teased her. Nor the others. She wouldn't mind anything if it meant they liked her, too.

"Did they show you the orchard yesterday?" asked Granny suddenly.

Prudy shook her head.

"Why don't you go now? It's pretty, and there's a little brook. You can wade if you like, but roll your pants above your knees, and don't stay in long. It's the spring branch—and cold."

Granny pointed out the path that led to the orchard. Prudy followed it through the tall grass. Soon she was under the fruit trees.

"Hi, Pigtails!"

The voice startled her. Prudy jumped.

"Up here, Pigtails!"

She looked up.

Spotty's freckled face grinned down from the branch of an apple tree.

So Spotty hadn't gone fishing at all! He might have taken her to the orchard himself. Prudy frowned.

"My name's not Pigtails."

"Why do you wear them, then?"

"I don't."

Spotty dropped from the branch into the grass beside her. He twitched a braid.

"You do. Look at this."

"They're pink-tails!"

"Pigtails, pigtails," chanted Spotty.

"Pink-tails, pink-tails," cried Prudy.

She stamped her foot.

Spotty laughed.

"Come on," he said suddenly. "Come with me, and I'll show you some pigtails—real ones."

"I don't want to."

"You don't dare. You know I'll prove yours *are* pigtails!"

"I do dare, too!"

"All right, then, come on."

Prudy came.

She followed Spotty back from the orchard, through the barn, and down a little hill.

At the bottom of the hill was a rail fence.

From behind the fence came a loud grunting sound and a strong, unpleasant smell.

Spotty boosted Prudy up until she could see over the top rail.

Prudy clung to the fence and stared.

Two great, ugly creatures stared back at her with wicked, twinkling little eyes. The third, a huge, dirty, yellow-white lump, lay in the mud, its back toward them. Its little stringy, curly tail was in full view.

"There you are," he said. "Pigtails. Yours are just like them."

"O-e-e-e-k," grunted one of the animals and put its snout back in a trough of horrid-looking food.

"Take a good look at their tails," Spotty said. "There's a fine set of pigtails for you!"

But Prudy had seen enough.

She slid down from the fence.

She wasn't going to cry. She *wouldn't* cry!

She started toward the house. She ran.

"Hey—hey, Prudy! Don't get mad, for goodness' sake!"

But Prudy wasn't listening. She only wanted to reach her room, her pretty little room, before the tears began. For now she knew she was going to cry—hard.

And she did.

She lay on her bed and cried a lot.

Then she got up and looked in the mirror above the little dressing table.

Her "pink-tails" were as smooth, as silver-gilt, or butter-colored, as ever. And Prudy knew that they didn't look at all like the tails on those great, horrid animals. But that Spotty, her favorite cousin, Spotty, should pretend they did made her very unhappy. He had laughed at her. He would tell the others. They would call her "Pigtails" and laugh at her.

And they had been so nice. Only yesterday they had been so kind.

Prudy peeped in the mirror again.

She wished she didn't have pink-tails, or pigtails. Anyway, she wished she didn't have them. She wished her hair were short. If her hair were short and she wore jeans, she'd look like a little boy. She could go fishing then, and maybe she could ride the pony as well as Midge did.

Prudy had an idea—an exciting one.

She tiptoed into Granny's room. No one was there.

In a moment, she tiptoed back and stood in front of the mirror again.

In her hand was a pair of long, sharp scissors.

Prudy lifted one of her pigtails and held it away from her head.

"Hi—Prudy!"

The scissors clattered on the floor, and Prudy turned around.

Spotty's face was peering in the window. He was in the big tree just outside. But he wasn't smiling now. He looked quite serious.

Prudy picked up the scissors.

"What are you doing?" asked Spotty.

"I—I'm going to cut them off—my pigtails."

Spotty crept a little nearer to the window.

"I wouldn't," he said quietly. "You know why? Well, you were right. Yours aren't pigtails at all— they're pink-tails. If you come on out, I'll show you some pink-tails."

"You won't! You'll take me back to see those awful pigs."

But Prudy put the scissors down.

"Not this time. I'll show you some pink-tails. You'll love them." Spotty smiled.

Prudy took a step toward the door.

"Okay?"

Prudy nodded.

"Meet me on the porch, then."

This time they went around the barn. They went down the little hill. Prudy could smell the pigs. She could hear them.

"O-e-e-ek, o-e-e-ek!"

But they went past the pen till they came to another fence. Spotty stopped. Prudy wrinkled her nose.

"It's still pigs," she said. "I can smell them!"

"E-e-e-e-k!" Such a funny, shrill baby squeal!

"Come on," Spotty said. "I'll give you a boost."

But Prudy was peering through the rails.

"Oh," she said, "aren't they the cutest things! Aren't they funny! Aren't they sweet!"

Prudy and Spotty climbed the fence together and sat side by side on top to watch the baby pigs.

There were ten of them. Ten active, playful little black-and-pink bodies, fat and glossy, with huge ears and tiny, mischievous eyes. They squealed and pushed and chased each other about the pen.

Prudy and Spotty watched and laughed.

"Oh, look! Look at that one!" cried Prudy.

"And look at *that* one," said Spotty. "Isn't he funny?"

"But look at the little pink one. Isn't he sweet?"

They laughed so hard they had to lean against each other.

Finally, they climbed down from the fence.

"Don't you like them?" asked Spotty.

"Yes. Oh, yes, they're darling!"

"Well, they've got *pink*-tails," said Spotty, "like yours. I was only teasing when I showed you the big pigs. Why, 'Pink-tails' is a nice nickname."

"Is Pink-tails—" Prudy stopped short. "Is Pink-tails a *nickname?*" she asked.

"Sure it is."

"Like Spotty? Or Midge? And will the others call me Pink-tails, too?"

"They will if I do. But if you don't like it—"

Prudy was suddenly happy, very happy. She was going to have a nickname like the others.

Spotty had been teasing her! What had Granny said? It showed he liked her. She would be one of them. Pink-tails or Pigtails, it didn't matter. Prudy grinned at her cousin.

"I like it a lot, Spotty," she said.

"Then that's okay. Say, you want to go fishing with us this afternoon, Pink-tails? We're all going, and I'll show you how—with my rod."

Prudy nodded. She was almost too happy to speak, but finally she said, "Okay, Spotty."

HIDDEN NEST

PRUDY LIKED STAYING AT MEADOWS FARM.
The summer days were long, and all sorts of
exciting things happened on each of them.

There was the rope swing that hung from
the branch of the tallest oak tree. Spotty swung
Prudy so high that he could run right under her;
so high that, for an instant, she was up among
the leaves; so high that she could see off and
away over the whole farm. It was fun!

Tommy and Tucker, who did everything
together, took Prudy wading in the brook.
And when her feet got so cold that her teeth
chattered, they all sat on the warm, grassy bank
and watched silly water spiders on the brown
stream—jumping, jumping all the time and never
getting anywhere.

Midge showed Prudy how to make friends with the animals.

There were so many animals!

Prudy loved the little brown-eyed calf and its mother.

"It's a heifer calf," Midge said. "It will grow up to be a Jersey cow and give lots of milk and never leave the farm."

Midge knew a lot.

Soon, the big farm horses pricked their ears when Prudy came into the barn and nickered softly, low in their throats.

Taffy, the gray pony, tossed his head and pawed the ground.

Prudy was sure to have a carrot or a sweet, juicy apple for each of them.

The dogs were fun, too. The spaniel, Bramble, went everywhere with the children. But Shep was a real farm dog and often too busy to play.

There were two cats. Sleek black Rastus lived at the barn. Miss Mouse was nearly always curled in the little old rocking chair in Granny's room.

"We usually have some kittens about the place," Granny said. "Miss Mouse has charming ones, mostly gray and like herself, with little white mittens."

"How lovely!" Prudy was helping feed the ducks. "I do like baby things, Granny, even baby pigs."

Granny set a pan of cracked corn carefully in a wire run.

"You should have seen these fellows about six weeks ago," she said as the young ducks crowded and jostled the pan. "Little balls of yellow fluff, they were. And their old mammy was so proud of them."

Granny sighed. "Young things grow too fast,"
she said. "They're at the awkward age now, and in
no time, they'll be fully grown."

"I'd love to see baby ducks," Prudy said. "They
must be darling. Oh, Granny, won't there be some
while I'm here?"

Granny looked thoughtful.

"It's late in the season, child," she said. "Most
baby creatures belong to the spring. But one of my

mammy ducks has hidden her nest away. I don't know where it is. She slips out to get her food before sunup, the silly thing. I must ask the boys to look for it. Now fetch that empty basket, Prudy, and we'll go back to the house."

Granny remembered about the nest. At lunchtime, she said, "What are you boys doing this afternoon?"

"Mom says we're to pick raspberries."

Aunt May looked up.

"I thought there were enough for supper," she said. "They're late this year. But if you want the boys for anything, Midge and I will do it."

"No," Granny said. "Tommy and Tucker can pick berries. It won't take long. And then all you children had better hunt for that hidden duck's nest. We're going to have rain, I know, and if those eggs are hatched in a storm, we may lose some good ducklings."

Prudy was puzzled.

"But Granny, I thought water was good for ducks. They like it, don't they? And they all swim."

"Not when they're tiny," Granny answered. "They shouldn't get wet until they've grown real feathers—they're all down at first, you know. And these are Muscovy ducks—some people call them dry land ducks. So," Granny laughed, "we'll have a real celebration this evening if someone finds that nest."

"I bet I know where it is," cried Midge.

"I bet *I* know where it is," cried Tommy.

And Spotty looked wise.

But Prudy hadn't the least idea where a mammy duck might hide her nest away.

~~~~~~

Tommy and Tucker waited on the back porch for baskets to put the berries in.

Prudy watched them.

"Is it hard to pick raspberries?" she asked. "I wish I could pick, too."

Tucker opened his mouth, but Tommy kicked his ankle, and he shut it again without saying anything.

"It isn't easy," Tommy said slowly. "You have to know the ripe ones, of course. But it's fun."

"Gee, yes!" Tucker said. He winked at Tommy.

"And when you've picked twenty berries, you get to eat one—the biggest in the basket."

"Couldn't I just come and help?"

"Can you count to twenty?" Tommy asked.

"Of *course* I can count to twenty. I can count to one hundred!"

"Swell! Shall we let her come, Tucker?"

"W-e-l-l, she might come with us. But do you think she ought to have a basket of her own? How about it, Pink-tails? Do you want a basket of your own? You have to fill it right up, you know."

Aunt May came out with the baskets.

"Pink-tails wants one, too, Mom," Tommy said. "She's going to help pick."

"That's nice," said Aunt May.

So Prudy followed the boys down the garden
path, swinging her basket proudly.

❦❦❦❦❦❦❦

The raspberry bushes were close by the old
latticed summer house.

The sun shone hot.

Among the green leaves were the ripe pink
berries.

The children began to pick.

One-two-three-four-five-six-seven—

Prudy popped a berry in her mouth. It was warm and sweet, the best she had ever tasted.

Picking *was* fun.

She picked on.

Tommy came around the bush at the end of the row. He looked into Prudy's basket and whistled.

"Good work, Pink-tails," he said. "You're a wonderful picker!"

"Yes, isn't she?" said Tucker, coming around the other side of the bush. "Why, she's much better than we are, Tommy. Look, she's half filled her basket already!"

Prudy was pleased. She wanted the boys to know it. They had been nice to let her come.

"You take some of mine," she said. And she emptied half her berries into Tommy's basket, half into Tucker's.

"Gee, Pink-tails, thanks!"

"I *love* to pick raspberries," Prudy said.

"Oh, anyone does," Tucker grinned.

"Yes," said Tommy, "we were lucky to get this job, weren't we? Spotty and Midge are combing burrs off the dogs."

Prudy started to fill her basket again.

The boys moved away, picking and laughing together.

Thirteen-fourteen-fifteen-sixteen-seventeen-eighteen—

Into Prudy's mouth went another ripe berry.

The sun was very hot.

Prudy's cheeks began to burn.

But she picked steadily. Once more the basket was half full.

One-two-three-four-five-six-seven—

It was very still. Prudy couldn't hear the boys anywhere. She wondered how many berries they had now. She would just go and see.

Prudy went around the row of berry bushes. No Tommy. No Tucker.

But there were two rows of bushes with an overgrown path between. They must be in there together. Prudy pushed through between the branches.

She was alone.

She looked for the boys' baskets. They were gone, too.

They *couldn't* have filled them in this time— not possibly. Then she remembered how she had divided her first lot of berries between the boys' two baskets.

Prudy got mad.

She remembered how the boys had laughed together. They had planned to leave her there, all alone! And they had gone off to look for the hidden duck's nest. That was it!

Prudy got madder.

She was hot. She was tired. Her cheeks burned like fire.

Prudy carried her basket of berries into the summer house. It was cooler there. She sat down

in the midst of the dust and the cobwebs and ate a
raspberry. And another. And another.

Suddenly, she stopped with a berry halfway to
her mouth.

What was that funny little noise?

A tiny chittering. A tiny cheeping. Then a
deeper note, answering back.

Prudy held her breath. She peeped through the
wooden lattice.

From under the floor of the old summer
house waddled a white mother duck. Around her
flitted and scurried a flock of tiny downy yellow
ducklings.

Prudy stared.

They must be from the hidden nest!

Granny should be told right away.

Prudy started for the house as hard as she could pelt. Rounding the bushes, she bumped into Spotty. Prudy went sprawling, and her basket of berries spilled all over the grass.

"Pink-tails, I'm sorry! But you were in an awful hurry, weren't you? Here, I'll help you pick up your berries." Spotty handed her the empty basket.

Prudy scrambled to her feet.

"Spotty," she gasped. "It's her! The—the mammy duck, and her babies are with her. They're like—like daffodils. Come on, I'll show you."

Together, and very quietly, Prudy and Spotty tiptoed back.

There was the white duck and her yellow brood.

"As proud as Punch," whispered Spotty. "But where did she have her nest, Pink-tails? Not in the raspberry bushes, was it? Tommy and Tucker would have found it, sure."

"I think—I think it was under the summer house. They—the boys—left me alone picking raspberries, and the mammy duck just walked out."

Spotty clapped a hand over his mouth.

"Oh, oh, oh! They're down at the barn! They're hunting everywhere! They've got Bramble helping them." Spotty stopped laughing. "But it serves them right for going off and leaving you to do the work."

He grabbed Prudy's hand.

"Come on, Pink-tails, come on and tell Gran you found the hidden nest."

Together they ran for the house.

Supper was a cheerful meal that evening.

Josie, who helped Granny in the kitchen, had baked a cake with white icing and a ring of rosy raspberries on top. In the center of the ring was a little yellow china duck.

"A gift for the girl who found the nest," said Granny. She scraped the icing off the pretty toy and put it at Prudy's place.

Prudy was delighted. "I'll keep it always, Granny," she said.

There was even vanilla ice cream. Aunt May had driven down to the village to get it.

"There weren't enough raspberries to go around," she said. "So we'll have them with our ice cream. They're delicious that way. It's funny, I thought there were a lot of berries on the bushes. But the boys only got a basketful between them."

"And Pink-tails spilled all of hers when she ran into me," said Spotty.

Tommy looked at Tucker.

Tucker looked at Tommy.

Tommy took his saucer and spilled the berries off into Prudy's ice cream.

Tucker did the same.

"Oh, oh, oh, thank you!" Prudy said. She picked up her spoon.

"And what do you think became of the berries Prudy spilled?" asked Granny.

They all looked at her.

"Every one of them got eaten by that sly old mammy duck!"

TREE HOUSE

PRUDY WAS IN THE BACKYARD, WATCHING HER baby ducks.

Everybody called them Pink-tail's ducks, since she had found the hidden nest. Granny let her give them their pan of grain, and the mother duck was so used to Prudy's voice and small, careful hand that she didn't mind when Prudy reached into the little wire run and picked up one of her fluffy yellow babies.

Prudy held it against her cheek for a moment and listened to its chittering. Granny said they were a fine, sturdy brood, and she would show them at the Hastings Fair.

Granny was going to show a pair of her Chinese geese, too. But Prudy didn't like the geese. She didn't like their long, snaky necks—nor the horrid way they crowded around and hissed. Prudy always made sure the geese were somewhere else when she went in to see the ducks.

Midge would walk right across the yard with the flock of big white geese at her heels.

"They won't hurt you," Midge said. "Well, they won't hurt me, anyway. One of them pinched me once, and do you know what I did? I took her around her silly neck and slapped her face—not hard, of course—but they know they aren't to pinch me again."

Prudy felt sure she could never, never slap a goose. She would rather just stay on the other side of the fence.

❦❦❦❦❦❦❦❦

"Pink-tails! Hey, Pink-tails!"

Someone was calling from the back porch.

Prudy put the yellow duckling back in the wire run and closed the trap door on top.

"Pink-*tails!*"

It was one of the boys.

Prudy answered, "Coming," and ran to the house.

"Look, Pink-tails, we're going to the Crow's Nest. Want to come with us?"

"Oh yes," said Prudy, because she always wanted to go everywhere with her cousins. "Where is it? Will there be baby crows in it?"

Spotty laughed. Prudy didn't mind when Spotty laughed at her. He was her favorite cousin.

But Tommy said, "Of course not, silly. The Crow's Nest is our tree house. Granny had it built three summers ago. It was a birthday present to all of us, and it's the best tree house in the world. We've got things inside, everything you need on a rainy day. There's—"

"Don't tell her," said Midge quickly. "It's always more fun when it's a surprise."

Prudy thought so, too, especially when she was going to see the surprise right away. She started with the others through the orchard, but the geese were there.

"I'll go around," Prudy said.

"I'll come, too, to show you the way," Tucker said.

The others were just latching the small gate between the orchard and the paddock when Prudy and Tucker got there.

In the corner of the paddock was a little grove of trees, and under one of them, the children stopped.

"There!" Tucker said proudly, looking up.

Prudy looked up, too.

Above her head, way above, set in the branches of a tree, was a little gray wooden house.

"How," asked Prudy in a very small voice, "how do you get up there?"

"You climb. Look, it's easy. We've got cleats nailed right on the tree. Only one's missing, and that's at the bottom. I'll boost you above that," said Spotty.

"Oh. Well, how—" asked Prudy in an even smaller voice, "how do you get down?"

"That's no trouble at all. You slide down the pipe, quicker than a wink."

"Pipe?" Prudy's voice was hardly more than a whisper. She looked. There was a long, long metal pipe from the tree house to the ground.

"Didn't you ever slide down anything?" asked Tommy. "You get a good grip with your hands and knees and just go. It's easy and fun."

Spotty looked at Prudy. She was very small, he thought. But Midge had been as small as that three summers ago when the Crow's Nest was new, and she had gone up the tall tree like a monkey! Midge had three brothers, though, and she'd climbed ever since she was a baby.

"Never mind about sliding down yet, Pink-tails," he said. "The first thing is to get you up there."

This was not easy. It was very, very difficult.

Tucker had already climbed to one of the lower branches. He sat there, telling them what to do. It didn't help.

Tommy went up several cleats and reached down a hand to Prudy. Spotty boosted from below. But Prudy's feet wouldn't go where she

wanted them to, and Tommy gripped her hand so hard her fingers ached.

"Don't look down," shouted Tucker. "That makes it worse!"

Midge stood some distance from the tree, holding Bramble by the collar. "I don't want her to fall on top of him," she said.

Both of Prudy's feet slipped at once. She stepped on Spotty's finger. There was an awful jerk, and for an instant, Prudy hung in midair. But Tommy didn't let go, and she caught hold of the next cleat below with her other hand.

"It's no good," Tommy gasped. "We'll just have to get her down again."

He and Spotty managed it between them.

PRUDY AT MEADOWS FARM

Prudy sat down, leaning against the tree, and looked at her arm. She'd scraped it quite badly on the rough bark when she'd slipped.

Spotty sucked the finger that Prudy had stepped on.

Midge and Tommy joined them, but Tucker went on up to the Crow's Nest.

"Too bad, Pink-tails," Spotty said at last.

Bramble licked her ear.

Midge was chewing on a blade of grass.

"I'll tell you what," she said. "It will just have to be Pink-tail's 'Special Scare.'"

"What—what's that?" asked Prudy. She was unhappy and still frightened. They had wanted her to see the Crow's Nest. She had wanted to see it herself. But she couldn't, simply couldn't, climb the tree. She swallowed hard and winked back tears.

"Well," said Midge, "a Special Scare is something you're afraid of. Mostly you have to get over being afraid of things, of course, but you can keep your Special Scare. If you *do* get over it, you can choose something else. And it's all right. The others can't even tease you about it. Mine's bats."

"Mine's spiders," said Tommy promptly.

Prudy looked at Spotty. If he had a Special Scare, she could certainly have one, too. But was Spotty afraid of anything?

"Mine's thunderstorms," Spotty said. "I know it's silly, and I don't show it much anymore, but I'm still scared of thunder and lightning."

Prudy felt better at once.

"Well, mine's going to be climbing that old tree," she said. "Or any other tree," she added quickly, in case the matter should come up again.

"All right, then, it's settled," said Midge.

As she spoke, the big bell at the house rang.

"Gee, that means they want one of us," Tommy said, getting up. "Or maybe all of us. We'd better all go, I guess."

Spotty lingered a moment.

"Coming, Pink-tails?" he asked.

Prudy shook her head.

"I—I think I'll stay awhile. I'll pick some daisies for Granny. There are lots down here."

"Okay." Spotty ran to catch up with the others, Bramble at his heels.

It was pleasant in the paddock. The sun was hot, but a breeze stirred the tall grasses, and the little singing insects were all about.

Prudy gathered an armful of yellow and white daisies and tall Queen Anne's lace.

Though Granny had a garden near the house, bright with old-fashioned flowers, she loved the ragged bunches of wild blossoms the children brought in from field and woodland. She filled brown and gray crocks and put them everywhere.

Above the hot, drowsy sound of the insects, Prudy could hear the clattering of the geese. They were in the orchard, she remembered. She reached for a lovely bunch of Queen Anne's lace. What loud voices geese had! Horrid things.

Prudy looked up.

The geese weren't in the orchard at all! They were in the paddock, coming straight for her!

Prudy's heart turned over.

She ran.

The geese scurried after her, clamoring. The gander spread his wings. Prudy could see them from the corner of her eye. She felt them at her heels. They might pinch her legs any minute!

Prudy reached the tree, the one that had the Crow's Nest in it.

She threw her flowers on the ground and scrambled up the cleats. She was breathless, but she was safe!

When she reached the lower branches, Prudy stopped and looked down. The geese were clustered below, eating her flowers.

"I thought you couldn't climb, Pink-tails."

Startled, Prudy looked up.

It was Tucker. She remembered then. Tucker hadn't gone to the house with the others. He'd been in the Crow's Nest all the time.

"Come on up," Tucker said. "It's nothing from there on. Here, I'll help you." He reached down a hand.

"I—I don't think you need to," Prudy said, for up among the branches it was easy. There was something to hold onto.

"There you are," Tucker said as Prudy reached the door of the little house. "Didn't I say it was the best tree house in all the world?"

It was.

It was roomy—for a tree house, anyway. A tight squeeze for four children, it was perfect for two. There was one little window with a wooden shutter and a door that would close. There was a shelf all the way around the walls, filled with books. When you sat on the floor, the books were nearly level with your eyes, making it easy to choose one. There was a bowl of red apples and a blue crock. When Tucker lifted the lid of the crock, Prudy saw that it was full of sugar cookies. Little tin boxes set in the shelves between the books held string, a knife, and a pair of pliers. To mend things, Tucker said. And there was a sturdy basket to be lowered with a rope for supplies. Yes, the Crow's Nest was perfect.

Prudy's eyes strayed along the line of books. Oh, there was one she knew! And there was the one about Pooh Bear, and *The Tailor of Gloucester*. Prudy pulled it out and looked at the pictures of the charming little mice.

Tucker settled against the wall with an apple and a battered copy of *Robin Hood*.

They were silent. They were happy.

An hour later, Tucker shook Prudy's shoulder. "Wake up, Dopey," he said.

Prudy blinked her eyes. Had she been asleep? Where was she?

"You ready to go?" Tucker asked. "It must be nearly supper time, and it's safe now. They're gone."

"Who's gone?" Prudy was only half awake yet.

"The geese, of course."

Prudy sat up and listened. She could hear the geese away off—probably in the duck yard.

"Did you go down and shoo them away?" she asked Tucker.

"I sure didn't! I leave that lot alone. Why, don't you know, Pink-tails? Geese are my Special Scare."

And Prudy remembered how he had come with her around the orchard—to show her the way.

"Climbing trees is mine," Prudy said.

"Not anymore, it isn't," Tucker told her. "You came up this tree like a kitten. I never saw anyone climb better."

Prudy felt rather proud.

"And now," said Tucker, "I'm going to show you how to get down—the easy way."

He uncoiled the long rope and made a small loop in the end with a knot that wouldn't come undone. Then he slid down the long pipe himself, not too fast, while Prudy watched carefully.

"You see how easy it is, Pink-tails?" Tucker said as he climbed up the tree again.

"Y-y-es."

Tucker made her put her foot in the loop of rope. He showed her how to grip the pipe with her hands and knees.

"You *can't* fall, Pink-tails," he said. "Not possible. And I'll keep you from going too fast with the rope. Now, when you're ready, you just say, 'Lower away.'"

Prudy gripped the pipe. She shut her eyes. "Lower away."

Down she went. Why, she *could* do it! Why, it was easy. Why—she was on the ground!

Down the pipe sailed Tucker.

The gate into the orchard was open. The others must have left it so when they went up to the house. That was how the geese had gotten into the paddock.

"Tucker," Prudy said suddenly, "could two people have the same Special Scare?"

"We never have had," said Tucker. "You see, I don't mind bats, nor spiders, nor thunderstorms. And the others don't mind geese."

"But I do, Tucker."

"That's right, Pink-tails. And you don't mind climbing trees anymore."

"I thought—I thought we might have geese for a Special Scare together." There was something friendly in the idea.

Tucker was silent a minute, thinking, then said, "Okay, Pink-tails, we'll share."

Prudy gave a little skip.

"Oh, thank you, Tucker," she said happily.

HASTINGS FAIR

Everyone at Meadows Farm was getting ready for the fair.

Granny had entered the family of ducklings and a pair of Chinese geese.

The Jersey cow would go, with her calf.

Josie was busy making her golden-brown cookies and a perfect chocolate cake. She wouldn't let the children set foot in the kitchen while the cake was in the oven for fear it would fall. But, for once, they weren't interested in the kitchen, not even when the lovely smell of baking cookies drifted through the house.

For the gray pony, Taffy, was going to the fair.

Midge was to ride him in the afternoon horse show.

"Why?" asked Prudy. She was watching Spotty as he combed out the pony's short, thick mane. "Why is *Midge* going to ride him?"

"Because she's the best rider in our family," Spotty said. "But we're all going to help, of course. Tommy's cleaning the saddle now, with saddle soap, and Tucker's doing the bridle. Do you want to help groom him?"

"Yes, oh, yes!"

Spotty handed Prudy a stiff brush and dragged up a wooden box for her to stand on so that she could reach the pony's back. Then he showed her how to brush the dust out of Taffy's gray coat.

Prudy felt very important.

"Is the horse show like the circus?" she asked Spotty.

Prudy's father had taken her to the great indoor circus when it came to the city last spring. She remembered the pretty ladies in bright costumes who stood tiptoe on big white horses as they circled around the ring. Surely Midge wouldn't be like that.

Just then Midge joined them. She was wearing a blue cotton shirt and strange looking pants, very wide above her knees and very tight below, with little straps that slipped under her brown shoes. Her face was serious.

Spotty grinned at her. "Pink-tails wants to know if the horse show will be like the circus."

"It won't," Midge said. "It won't because you just sit and look at the circus, but you're *in* a horse show. You are part of it. And you try awfully hard to ride better than you ever have before." She pulled an apple out of her pocket, took a bite, and gave the rest to Taffy, who jerked his head up and down approvingly.

"But the others won't be riding, will they?" asked Prudy.

"No, but they'll be watching and wanting me to win. It's just as hard."

Tommy and Tucker came up with the saddle and bridle, all spotlessly clean.

"Let's take him up to the high field now," Midge

said, slipping the bridle over the pony's head, "and let's make the field like the one at the fair as much as we can."

"How can we do that?" asked Tommy. "You can't make Taffy think that three people—four, with Pink-tails—are a crowd. And we haven't any music. There's sure to be music at the fair."

"Oh dear." Midge looked more serious than ever. "I suppose we wouldn't dare borrow Dad's portable radio without asking. And they won't let us if we do ask. Well, there are some balloons up at the house. Get those, Tommy. You and Pink-tails can run about under his nose with them and yell, anyway."

"And get trodden on, I suppose," snorted Tommy.

"Oh, no! Horses don't like to tread on people. He might just kick at you as he goes by, but I'll soon cure him of that," said Midge firmly. "We'll take the dogs, too, to make more of a crowd. And Spotty can shout orders, when to change gait and reverse and all that. It's bound to help some."

Midge gathered up her reins, Spotty gave her a boost into the saddle, and she trotted off toward the high field.

The others whistled for the dogs, blew up the balloons, and followed.

They spent the rest of the morning there, running and shouting and getting very hot

indeed. Midge rode the pony in big circles and small circles and figure eights. She trotted and cantered as Spotty directed. Prudy's blue balloon got away from her and bounded right under Taffy's feet, where it exploded with a loud pop. He shied, but Midge never minded at all. Surely, Prudy thought, surely no one at the horse show could ride better than her cousin Midge.

The gray pony was dark with sweat, and
Midge's short hair lay wet against her pink face
before they heard the distant bell calling them to
dinner.

They rested in the afternoon. They lay in the
grass on the shady lawn and worried about the
weather. It wouldn't—it couldn't—rain for Fair Day.

Nor did it.

Morning dawned, clear and bright, with the gentlest of breezes and bluest of skies.

Everyone was up early.

Spotty and Midge left soon after sunup, in the farm truck, with Taffy and the Jerseys.

It was a tight squeeze for the others in Granny's station wagon, along with the crate of ducklings, Josie's cake and cookies and jars of preserves, and their own picnic lunch in a big wicker basket.

Tucker had brought Bramble.

"He's never been to the fair," Tucker said. "I promised him he could go this year. I'll keep him on a leash while I show him everything, and after that, he can wait for us in the car. I know he'll be good."

"And I know he won't," said Gran. Bramble looked at her. Tucker looked at her. "But if you'll be responsible for him all day, Tucker…" So Bramble went to the fair.

The station wagon moved slowly along the road.

Ahead of them rumbled a big farm wagon half
filled with hay. In it sat an old woman with wild
gray hair and sharp little eyes.

"Gran!" shouted Tommy. "Look! Four yoke!
Aren't they beauties?"

Sure enough, the wagon was drawn by eight
huge red-and-white oxen. Beside the leaders
walked a lean old man with a long, long whip. He
flicked the oxen and shouted, crowding them over
so Gran could get the station wagon by.

"Good morning, Mr. Newton," she called.
"Good luck! Good luck at the fair!"

A car turned in from a side road. In the back
seat, peering out the window, were two brown-
and-white goats!

They passed a tall man on a tall bay horse, which danced a little on the grassy edge of the road as the rider touched his hat to Gran and smiled at the children.

All were on their way to Hastings Fair.

Spotty and Midge joined them at the fairgrounds. This was a pretty, rolling field, partly shaded by oak trees. Farthest from the road, the land dipped down to a grassy level space. A low wall surrounded it, topped by a white painted fence.

"That's where they have the horse show," said Midge, shading her eyes with her hand.

Prudy shaded her eyes and looked, too, but the level place was empty, and on top of the hill, under the trees, all was bustle and excitement. People were milling about, children underfoot, animals everywhere. And such a noise! There was indeed music—loud, raucous music—but beneath it, you heard the lowing of cows, the bleating of sheep, and occasionally the distant shrill whinny of a horse. Only the big red oxen stood silent, patient, their necks low under their heavy wooden yokes, waiting for their work to begin.

"They have pulling contests with them," Spotty told Prudy. "I've seen one yoke move a sledge load of rocks that weighed 3,000 pounds! They're awfully strong—but not very smart."

"Let's go see where they've put the Jersey," Tucker said.

Tommy wanted to wait till the cattle were being judged.

"We could go to the Fun Fair first," he said. "They've got swings, big wooden ones like boats. They almost turn over, they go so high. And there's a shooting gallery and a merry-go-round."

Prudy hadn't known what she wanted to do, only to see everything, to go everywhere. But now she knew.

"Oh, let's!" she cried. "Do let's go on the merry-go-round!" She clapped her hands and jumped up and down. "Don't *you* want to go, Spotty? Don't *you* want to, Midge?"

Spotty laughed at her eagerness.

Midge kicked a pebble out of her way.

"A merry-go-round!" she said, frowning. "No, I don't want anything to do with it. I ride real horses, not wooden ones." And she slipped away through the crowd.

Prudy felt as if she'd been slapped.

"I think Midge is perfectly horrid!" she said.

"Midge is rather a pest when she's scared," said Spotty. "She'll be like that till after the horse show."

"Scared! But what's she scared of?" asked Prudy. "She isn't scared of Taffy; she rides him all the time."

"Oh, she isn't afraid of the pony. She isn't afraid of any horse. It's just … well, she's afraid she won't do her best. And she's sort of riding for all of us, you see."

"I still think she's horrid," Prudy said. "And maybe, maybe I won't go to her old horse show either! I don't have to, do I, Spotty?"

"Suit yourself, Pink-tails. But we'll back her up, of course, no matter how she behaves. She's our sister."

Spotty, too, disappeared in the crowd.

Prudy trailed Tommy and Tucker around the fairgrounds all morning.

They rode on the merry-go-round, but one of them always had to wait outside holding Bramble. It wasn't much fun.

The swing-boats made Prudy feel giddy.

Tommy won a prize at the shooting gallery, a plaster dwarf painted green. He said Gran would love it and went off to put it in the car.

Tucker and Prudy and Bramble looked at the lambs and the goats. The kids were charming and could climb anywhere. Prudy laughed and laughed as a young farmer scooped a pair off the rock wall, one under each arm, and carried them back to the pen, only to have them scramble out again the minute his back was turned.

"I wish we had goats at the farm," she said to Tucker. "They're so cute."

"So do I," Tucker agreed. "Let's ask Gran to get a pair, shall we?"

At lunchtime, Granny was in a mood to promise anything, for she'd done well with her entries. The Jersey heifer had taken a first prize, the duck family a third. Josie's chocolate cake was a blue ribbon winner. She was so pleased.

"It's our day!" Gran said, smiling. "And I know you'll do nicely with the pony this afternoon, Midge. He goes well for you, child."

Midge said thank you in a strange little voice, but she never said another word. She ate one sandwich and went off with Aunt May before the others had finished lunch.

"You'd better not come to the stables, Pink-tails," Spotty told Prudy. "I'll be helping, and it's crowded. You might get kicked or stepped on."

"I *wasn't* coming!"

She wasn't going to their old horse show, either, Prudy thought.

But somehow, by mid-afternoon, her feet took her to that grassy, level space. There was a big

crowd all the way around it, and she was on the
wrong side, with the sun in her eyes. Two men
in riding clothes were sitting in a little patch of
shade on the bank. One of them smiled at her and
made room beside him. Prudy sat down and said,
"Thank you."

There were a great many riders in the ring,
some on horses and some on ponies, trotting
round and round. Then she saw Midge and Taffy
among them! How nice Midge looked, Prudy
thought. She was wearing a white shirt today and
a little round felt hat the color of her funny pants.
And how nice Taffy looked, too, arching his neck
and picking his feet up smartly.

A loud voice shouted, "Walk, please," and all
the horses slowed down.

"Reverse and canter!" They all turned about
and went in the other direction. All except one
small boy on a very stubborn pony that pulled
its head down and wouldn't turn at all. But how
promptly Midge had gotten Taffy around. How

smoothly he cantered along, in and out among the other riders!

A red balloon, loosed by some child in the crowd, drifted out across the ring, right among the horses. A brown-and-white pony stood straight up on its hind legs, and the boy who was riding it slid off over its tail! Someone caught the pony, and the boy was back in the saddle at once, but Prudy thought, "That might have been Midge. I'm glad—oh, I'm glad we got Taffy used to balloons yesterday." Why, she had helped. She had helped a little to train the pony. Though, of course, Midge was doing the hard part. Prudy looked again at Midge and Taffy out there in the ring. Suddenly, she felt very proud of them both.

The riders were told to "Line up, now." Then more than half of them rode away, up the hill toward the stables.

But Midge and Taffy stayed. They trotted once more around the ring, cantered in a figure eight, alone, came to a stop, and backed up a few steps. Other riders did the same, then lined up again.

"That's a very nice Welsh pony." One of the men beside Prudy was speaking. "And the kid knows how to handle him. She'll make a real rider one of these days."

"It wouldn't surprise me if she got the reserve," said the other man. "Yes, there she goes."

Midge and Taffy moved up to second place in the line, behind an older girl on a handsome black horse.

"Who is the child, anyway? But they'll announce it in a minute, of course."

Prudy couldn't wait that minute. She was on her feet, bursting with pride.

"I know," she said. "I know who she is! She's my cousin Midge—Midge Meadows."

"Of Meadows Farm? Well, young lady, you can tell your cousin that she did a very nice bit of riding today. Tell her Major Ross says so. And you might add that's a really good pony she's got. They go well together, those two."

"Oh, thank you, Major Ross!"

The loudspeaker was blaring.

"Results of the Class in Horsemanship: first, Miss Sally Pendleton. Second—and reserve—Miss Midge Meadows."

But Prudy hardly heard, for she was wriggling through the crowd, running up the hill toward the stables.

Spotty was there, and just as she reached him, Midge cantered up. Her eyes were shining, her cheeks flushed, her mouth one wide smile. She slid to the ground and threw her arms around

the pony's neck. She hugged Spotty. She hugged
Prudy. Tommy, Tucker, and Bramble raced up the
hill, followed more slowly by Gran and Aunt May.
Midge hugged them all.

"Wasn't Taffy *wonderful*?" she kept saying. "He
was so *good*! He did everything I wanted him to—
every single thing!"

"You were wonderful, too." It was Prudy's
chance to speak. "Major Ross said so. He said—"

"Major Ross!" Midge whispered. "Did he speak to you? But he's a marvelous rider, Pink-tails, the best anywhere around here. He shows hunters."

"Oh, yes, I watched the horse show with Major Ross. He asked who you were, and I told him, and he said you were awfully good and—and that you and Taffy went well together. I was to tell you so from him."

"Gee!" Tommy and Tucker said, in one breath.

Midge's eyes filled with tears, but she was smiling at the same time.

"Oh, oh! Thank you, Pink-tails, for telling me. I just *never* was so happy!" She wiped her tears away with a rather smudgy hand. "And I never was so hungry, either. I want a hot dog with lots of mustard and some of that pink cotton candy on a stick. And then, I'll tell you what we should do—" Midge paused.

Sweet and distant, they could hear the music from the Fun Fair.

"Let's all go and ride on the merry-go-round! Don't *you* want to, Pink-tails?"

Prudy stood in front of the big mirror in Granny's room while Granny tied the strings of her crisp white pinafore over her little blue dress. For Mother and Daddy were coming, and this was how Daddy liked to see her look. But Prudy felt as strange, almost, as she had the first time she'd put on blue jeans. Her skin was browned by wind and sun. There was a dark bruise on one knee, a long scraped place on her arm, and a red patch from

poison ivy on her hand. Would Daddy think her like sugar and spice now, Prudy wondered? Would he say she was sweet enough to eat? Only her pink-tails were the same, still butter-colored, or silver-gilt. She was glad Spotty hadn't let her cut them off. Prudy smiled. Spotty was her favorite cousin still.

"There!" Granny said suddenly. "Isn't that the car turning in the gate now? Run, child, run!"

Prudy ran.

It was wonderful to see Mother and Daddy again.

And they stayed overnight.

Everybody sat before a little fire in the living room after supper. It was cozy, their first cool evening.

"Prudy," said her father, "I do believe you've grown!"

"And she looks so well," said her mother.

"Oh, the country's done her good. I thought she was a little wispy when she came." Granny smiled.

"She didn't know much, and she couldn't do anything, then," Tommy said. "Remember, Pink-tails, when you couldn't even climb a tree?"

"She climbs like a monkey now," said Spotty.

"And she rides the pony without being led. She didn't fall off at all yesterday, did you, Pink-tails?"

"She can walk the old footlog across the creek."

"And run almost as fast as Midge can now."

Prudy sighed. It had all been such fun.

"Maybe Granny will let you come again."

"Again—and soon," said Granny.

"And maybe Granny will let us come, too," Daddy said.

"Oh, do come!" the children cried. "Come, gather nuts in the fall."

"Come for Thanksgiving!"

"Come for Christmas! There might be skating on the Mill Pond by then."

"Skating!" cried Prudy. "Oh, Daddy, you could teach me to skate."

"I could," Daddy agreed. "I will." He smiled across at Mother. "But you'll have to get some sturdy clothes for our tomboy daughter. Overalls—snowsuits—something of that sort."

Mother looked demurely at the toes of her own pretty slippers.

"Perhaps you're right, dear," she said.

THE END

More Books from The Good and the Beautiful Library

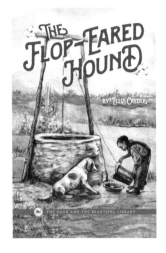

The Flop-Eared Hound
by Ellis Credle

Brian's Victory
by Ethel Calvert Phillips

Mpengo of the Congo
by Grace W. McGarran

Calico
by Ethel Calvert Phillips

www.goodandbeautiful.com